Grandma Rabbitty's Visit

Barry Smith

Grandma Rabbitty is coming to visit today!

No, Grandma Rabbitty is not on the bus!

Clunketta, clacketta, clank!

Is this Grandma Rabbitty?

Nhhmm...

No! Grandma Rabbitty doesn't drive a tractor!

Tinkle, tinkle, tinkle.

Could this be Grandma Rabbitty?

No! But it's the ice cream truck. Yummy!

R-r-rahr-r-r-r! R-r-rahr-r-r-r!
This must be Grandma Rabbitty!

Of course not! She doesn't ride on a fire engine!

Kerchunk, kerchunk, **crrunch!**

This can't be Grandma Rabbitty.

She doesn't drive a steamroller!

Putt, putt, putt.

Here she comes!

No, that's not Grandma Rabbitty in the sports car!

Vroom, vroom, vroooom . . .

Who's this on the motorbike?